THIS IS ME! ACROSTICS

Treasured Words

Edited By Allie Jones

First published in Great Britain in 2022 by:

Young Writers
Remus House
Coltsfoot Drive
Peterborough
PE2 9BF
Telephone: 01733 890066
Website: www.youngwriters.co.uk

All Rights Reserved
Book Design by Ashley Janson
© Copyright Contributors 2022
Softback ISBN 978-1-83928-608-7

Printed and bound in the UK by BookPrintingUK
Website: www.bookprintinguk.com
YB0519D

Foreword

Welcome Reader,

For Young Writers' latest competition *This Is Me Acrostics*, we asked primary school pupils to look inside themselves, to think about what makes them unique, and then write an acrostic poem about it! They rose to the challenge magnificently and the result is this fantastic collection of poems, celebrating them and the things that are important to them.

Here at Young Writers our aim is to encourage creativity in children and to inspire a love of the written word, so it's great to get such an amazing response, with some absolutely fantastic poems. It's important for children to focus on and celebrate themselves and this competition allowed them to write freely and honestly, celebrating what makes them great, expressing their hopes and fears, or simply writing about their favourite things. *This Is Me Acrostics* gave them the power of words.

I'd like to congratulate all the young poets in this anthology, I hope this inspires them to continue with their creative writing.

Contents

Independent Entries

Ava Pearson-Rudd (7)	1

Beechwood Primary Academy, Southway

Lily Mills (11)	2
Ellie Mills (11)	3
Sarah Cretch (10)	4

Krishna Avanti Primary School, Evington

Charles Blower Hamilton (6)	5
Joshua De Hoedt (7)	6
Aarohi Rajput (7)	7
Navaneeth Mundalappa (7)	8
Niyam Ramji (7)	9
Drashtiba Parmar (7)	10
Vrinda Mathur (7)	11
Krishang Joshi (7)	12
Aarav Parmar (6)	13
Krishiv Nair (7)	14
Alisha Bamal (7)	15
Krsangi Vishaka Dasi (7)	16
Krshnavi Nair (7)	17
Nirupama Rajeev (7)	18
Darshji Odedra (7)	19
Khyat Kothari (7)	20
Krish Thanky (6)	21
Kush Raichura-Tailor (7)	22
Jasneet Braich (7)	23
Raghav Sharma (6)	24
Ava-Maya Patel (6)	25
Kavya Odedra (7)	26
Parina Odedra (7)	27
Aaryan Kapadia (6)	28
Varunavi Joshi (7)	29
Yash Pankhania (7)	30
Hitarth Briiesh (7)	31
Viaan Mehta (7)	32
Navraj Sharma (7)	33
Jia Kang (7)	34
Jessica Ramji (6)	35
Parth Karavadra (7)	36
Armanvir Singh (7)	37
Anita Guntuboyina (6)	38
Shreya Tank (6)	39
Aaron Bharakhada (6)	40
Arman Singh Bhatti (7)	41
Olivia Blower-Hamilton (6)	42
Diwan Yogendra (7)	43
Jaanav Desai (7)	44
Anaiya Mistry (7)	45
Dhruvi Patel (6)	46
Kiana Mamtora (7)	47
Priya Goraniya (7)	48
Amelia Venugopalan (6)	49
Mavleen Kaur (7)	50
Kaiyah Jasmine Patel (6)	51
Raina Bhundia (6)	52
Tulsi Barot (7)	53
Mylo Vekaria (7)	54
Raj Keshvala (6)	55

Marjorie McClure School, Chislehurst

Austin Hughes (10)	56
Cassandra Weallans (10)	57
Taylor Blake (8)	58

Montreal CE Primary School, Cleator Moor

Saskia Freeman (5)	59
Lucy Gearing (6)	60
Amelia Nicholson (7)	61
Bella Freeman (6)	62
Keelan Connolly (7)	63
Quinn Beeson (6)	64
Freya Jennings (7)	65
Seth Faragher (6)	66
Isla Devine (7)	67
Harry Cope (5)	68
Darcey McCall (6)	69
Ella Gauld (4)	70
Brooke Donnell (7)	71
Rosa-Mai Rice (7)	72
Esmae-Rose Dawson (5)	73
George Rigg (4)	74
Oakley Pattinson (5)	75
Evie Dalton (5)	76
James Finch (7)	77
Lola Adams (5)	78
Reggie Graham (4)	79

St Paul's CE Primary School, Winchmore Hill

Katie Nelson (7)	80
Sarah Carlotti (7)	81
Isabelle Ellis (7)	82
Vheer Vaswani (6)	83
Jacob Kalu (6)	84
Phoebe Christofedou (7)	85
Elizabeth Roberts (7)	86
Joseph Coombes (7)	87
Milo Albery (6)	88
Ezekiel Cawood (7)	89
Teddy Hale (6)	90
Mia Ellis (7)	91
Emma Nelson (7)	92
Austin Reeves (7)	93
Iris Lim (7)	94
Josh Jagpal (7)	95

Alexander Scott (7)	96
Finn Davies (7)	97
Holly Bennett (6)	98
Aston Agyekum (7)	99
Luke Mournehis (5)	100
Nell Taheny (7)	101

The White House Preparatory School, London

Noah Kessler (7)	102
Edward Kelsey (7)	103
Francesca Lombardi-Werner (7)	104
Zixi Jian (7)	105
Nate Sanger (7)	106
Iris Adeusi (7)	107
Ajit Nair (7)	108
Henry Gaunt (7)	109
Oliver Xu (7)	110
Zara Watt (7)	111
Jai McKenzie (7)	112
Mia Aggarwal (7)	113

Wold Newton Foundation School, Wold Newton

Tia Marley (7)	114
Millie Worrell (7)	115
Noah Pinder (7)	116
Barnaby Elston (7)	117
Isabelle Hunter (7)	118
Chloe Warters (6)	119
Alban Joyce (7)	120
Harvey Hart (7)	121
Florence Scott (7)	122

Ysgol Ffordd Dyffryn, Llandudno

Sophie Hender (6)	123
Elodie Evans (6)	124
Azra Gayrak (6)	125
Louie Thomas (6)	126
Niamh Foster (6)	127
Christopher Jones-Gallagher (6)	128

Eliza Trow (5)	129
Alanur Gurel (5)	130
Alice Cruse (6)	131
Demi Shingler (6)	132
Mya Griffiths (6)	133
Harlem Williams (6)	134

The Acrostics

Sushi

S alty soy sauce tingling on my tongue
U nusual texture of the bobbly nori and the squishy tuna
S mells of the sea wafting into my nose
H andmade with care, perfection and precision
I take a bite and it feels like I am on a river in Japan.

Ava Pearson-Rudd (7)

Heartstrings

H eartstrings a compassionate feeling to family and friends,
E ven if you no longer feel it, your love never ends,
A nd heartstrings, the feeling must never be broken,
R emember to always cherish your love as a prize or token,
T o be honest with you, heartstrings make me smile,
S ayings that I should tell you my heartstrings stretch a mile,
T hanks to you and thanks to myself,
R apid darting love you send to yourself,
I gnore the hate and bring in the pride,
N ext to each other we stand, side to side,
G etting your attention again, my heartstrings stand high and tall,
S o I love my heartstrings because it means I love you most of all.

Lily Mills (11)
Beechwood Primary Academy, Southway

My Sister Lily

M y sister is very annoying you know
Y ou don't know the pain I listen to

S he moans on the way home
I can't even use her pens, you will never ever know
S he has a bad temper, almost every day
T he things I do for her and she says I'm okay
E ven though we fight
R eally she can be chilled

L ily gets on my nerves
I know her love is still bright
L ily and I are twins, we are different though
Y ou know we hate each other and love each other.

Ellie Mills (11)
Beechwood Primary Academy, Southway

Christmas Joy

C andy canes and carols,
H anging decorations all around,
R udolph the reindeer,
I cy and cold,
S now all around,
T ime with family,
M ince pies in the oven,
A ngel sitting atop the tree,
S anta Claus,

J ingle bells playing,
O pening presents,
Y ule log.

Sarah Cretch (10)
Beechwood Primary Academy, Southway

Teddy Bear

T eddy is the best
E rm, I do not know what to do today, let's ask Teddy
"D o a flip," I told Teddy
"D o the splits," Teddy told me
"Y ou are the best, Teddy," I replied

B est is best, Teddy knows best
E ddy is Teddy's best friend
A bear is not nice most times but Teddy is always nice
R iding on Charles is so much fun!

Charles Blower Hamilton (6)
Krishna Avanti Primary School, Evington

Minecraft

M inecraft is my favourite mind-blowing game
I t inspires me to play every day
N aturistic game that has naturistic animals
E xciting things feature in the game
C raft-efficient tools and sharp weapons to fight
R aft so you can sail to sea
A mazing pictures
F arm food so you can survive
T hrilling game so beware of zombies, they're everywhere.

Joshua De Hoedt (7)
Krishna Avanti Primary School, Evington

Swimming

S wimming is really fun!
W hen it was the first day of swimming I was really shy, but when I tried it it was fun.
I always go swimming on Thursday with my dad.
M y swimming teacher put me in stage 2 swimming.
M y friend Aary tried swimming one time.
I am on stage 2 swimming.
N ow I like swimming.
G oats and cats don't like water or swimming.

Aarohi Rajput (7)
Krishna Avanti Primary School, Evington

Minecraft

M ob of doom is scary
I nteractive building is fun
N ice coloured pixel
E xciting things, even portals
C raft is cool and it makes me happy
R esilient crafts and you can make things with blocks
A mazing pictures, even zombies
F ighting is hard and you have to kill mobs
T hrilling game.

Navaneeth Mundalappa (7)
Krishna Avanti Primary School, Evington

Monkey

M agic monkeys eat bananas because they like them and they're addictive
O ranges are healthy for them, but they do not like them
N aughty they are, very naughty, especially when people visit
K ing monkey likes to play hide-and-seek
E at bananas all day
Y oung monkeys sleep fast and wake up early.

Niyam Ramji (7)
Krishna Avanti Primary School, Evington

Happiness

H appy every day
A lways everyone is happy
P eople are always happy
P layful because we have happiness in us
I t is good to have happiness
N ever to be sad, always happy
E veryone has happiness in them
S uper excited to have happiness
S it with friends and be happy.

Drashtiba Parmar (7)
Krishna Avanti Primary School, Evington

Gymnastics

G ym is the best, I will tell you
Y ou will have lots of fun
M y gym is the best
N ow you will be fit
A nd you will like it
S o many teachers to help
T o teach us the press ups
I want to go forever
C ome and have fun
S o you will be strong.

Vrinda Mathur (7)
Krishna Avanti Primary School, Evington

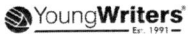

Mrs Marshal

M akes friends
R espectful
S he's always on our side

M akes friends with teachers
A nyone should be grateful for her
R eady for a fun trip
S he's always nice
H elpful
A lways ready for a fun trip
L oves cherry tomatoes.

Krishang Joshi (7)
Krishna Avanti Primary School, Evington

Football

F ouls are in football
O n Saturday I go to play matches
O nly our team is allowed to play
T eams win, sometimes lose
B alls, goals, score
A goalie can pick up the ball
L eft is the goalie's weakness
L et's go and play football.

Aarav Parmar (6)
Krishna Avanti Primary School, Evington

Sports

S wimming is a thing.
P laying I enjoy.
O lympic sportsman is what I want to become.
R unning fast as I go, let's go play some sports.
T oo hot, too cold? No problem!
S ports is not about winning it is about having fun.

Krishiv Nair (7)
Krishna Avanti Primary School, Evington

Ballet

B allet is so peaceful
A relaxing class is so nice
L ie on your mat for a warm-up, it is just a dream
L eg warm-ups feel so active that I can jump
E ee, a good stretch feels good
T oo easy, give me some hard moves.

Alisha Bamal (7)
Krishna Avanti Primary School, Evington

Krsangi

K rsangi is kind
R ainbow are her favourite colours
S unshine is the best
A mazing Chocolate and Flake
N ervous about maths
G oing on adventures
I maginative when she goes to sleep.

Krsangi Vishaka Dasi (7)
Krishna Avanti Primary School, Evington

Flowers

F lowers are beautiful
L eaves come out in autumn
O ctober is a month
W atering plants is so much fun
E xpired food is disgusting
R oots are so hard to pull out
S ilence is calming.

Krshnavi Nair (7)
Krishna Avanti Primary School, Evington

Swimming

S plashing is fun!
W arm as a hot tub
I nteresting
M arvellous
M om likes swimming
I t's relaxing
N ervous when I go swimming
G ames in the swimming pool are fun.

Nirupama Rajeev (7)
Krishna Avanti Primary School, Evington

Sports Day

S ometimes I get sweaty playing sports
P owerful and gives me energy
O lympic medals I'd love to win
R unning is part of sports
T ennis is my favourite sport
S ports are my favourite.

Darshji Odedra (7)
Krishna Avanti Primary School, Evington

Holiday

H aving a good time
O ctober is when I go
L ike holidays because they are fun
I like holidays
D ays on holiday are nice to relax
A relaxing holiday
Y ay, having new friends.

Khyat Kothari (7)
Krishna Avanti Primary School, Evington

Ronaldo

R olls Royce
O ne of the best footballers
N ever ever giving up
A lways running fast
L oves his team Manchester Utd
D oing everything he can do
O ne of the top 5 footballers.

Krish Thanky (6)
Krishna Avanti Primary School, Evington

Monkeys

M onkeys are my favourite
O ranges are healthy for animals
N aughty
K ick other monkeys when they snatch their food
E very monkey likes swinging
Y oung baby monkeys like bananas.

Kush Raichura-Tailor (7)
Krishna Avanti Primary School, Evington

Flowers

F un to play with
L eafy but not a leaf
O pens up peacefully
W ater has to be sprayed on them
E veryone likes flowers
R oses are my favourite
S o go get flowers.

Jasneet Braich (7)
Krishna Avanti Primary School, Evington

Raghav

R aghav makes me feel very special
A lways love my friends
G uava juice is my favourite YouTuber
H eroes are my favourite
A aron is my friend
V enom is my favourite movie.

Raghav Sharma (6)
Krishna Avanti Primary School, Evington

Cooking Is Good

C hocolate is my favourite
O ats are good for you
O ranges are healthy
K inder eggs are yummy
I ce cream is cold
N obody likes rice
G ood food helps us grow.

Ava-Maya Patel (6)
Krishna Avanti Primary School, Evington

Swimming

S plashing
W ater
I like to dive
M y floaty is beautiful
M y costume is pink
I love waves
N o food allowed in the swimming pool
G ames are fun.

Kavya Odedra (7)
Krishna Avanti Primary School, Evington

Singing!

S inging makes me happy
I love singing because it is fun
N ice to hear
G reat at singing
I like the beats
N otes are calming to me
G reat at vocals.

Parina Odedra (7)
Krishna Avanti Primary School, Evington

All About Me

A nimals, fat, chubby, cute
A nts make me tickle and itch
R eading is my best hobby
Y o-yos make me happy
A ryana is my little sister
N o I don't eat meat.

Aaryan Kapadia (6)
Krishna Avanti Primary School, Evington

All About Varunavi's Hobby

V ery helpful
A lways creative
R eally active
U nlikely to be last
N ot unkind
A lways courageous
V ery brave
I 'm very strong.

Varunavi Joshi (7)
Krishna Avanti Primary School, Evington

Golf Shots From Yash

G olf is fun
O ver bridges
L oft
F lop shots

S cores
H itting a shot
O nto greens
T ee shots
S ick shots!

Yash Pankhania (7)
Krishna Avanti Primary School, Evington

All About Me

H itarth is smart
I t's a nice day
T rading Pokémon cards
A fast person
R eally good
T rying new games
H itarth is shy.

Hitarth Briiesh (7)
Krishna Avanti Primary School, Evington

Sports

S trong because you build confidence
P erfect workout
O nly sports make you fast
R unning is fun
T rying sports is fun
S lim and sporty.

Viaan Mehta (7)
Krishna Avanti Primary School, Evington

Playing

N ice playing with my brother
A mazing to play
V ery nice to play
R olling the ball
A mazing tricks
J urassic World play with dinosaurs.

Navraj Sharma (7)
Krishna Avanti Primary School, Evington

I Love Dance

D oing dance makes me active
A lways puts a smile on my face
N ow I will show my family
C ourage come in my body
E motional dance is my favourite.

Jia Kang (7)
Krishna Avanti Primary School, Evington

Teddy

T iny and medium in size
E ars are soft and cuddly
D ogs look like teddy bears
D efinitely I love teddies
Y ay, I love it as much as my sisters.

Jessica Ramji (6)
Krishna Avanti Primary School, Evington

Parth

P laying Minecraft with my sister.
A vengers is my favourite movie.
R iya plays with me.
T attoos of Sonic on my arm.
H orrid Henry is funny.

Parth Karavadra (7)
Krishna Avanti Primary School, Evington

Armanvir

H aving a new toy
A nice person being helpful
P ranking your friends with their permission
P izza makes you happy
Y ou are happy and nice.

Armanvir Singh (7)
Krishna Avanti Primary School, Evington

Anita

A nita is so kind
N ails are beautiful
I ce cream is my favourite food
T ea and biscuits I eat at breakfast
A pples are yummy and tasty.

Anita Guntuboyina (6)
Krishna Avanti Primary School, Evington

Mudaf

M udaf is yummy
U se it every day and drink it every day
D elicious and yummy!
A ctually yummy and brilliant
F un and extraordinary.

Shreya Tank (6)
Krishna Avanti Primary School, Evington

All About Me

A lways like playing with my sister
A lways active
R oadtrips are super
O n the iPad
N ice and like to play hide-and-seek and tag.

Aaron Bharakhada (6)
Krishna Avanti Primary School, Evington

All About Happy

H appy is the best feeling
A happy feeling is the best feeling
P eace and quiet
P eace in the world
Y es, it is relaxing.

Arman Singh Bhatti (7)
Krishna Avanti Primary School, Evington

Olivia

O livia likes pets
I like food
L ove my mum
V ans are medium size
I love to go to the park
A bee is yellow.

Olivia Blower-Hamilton (6)
Krishna Avanti Primary School, Evington

Diwan

D iwan is my name
I love my school
W e have lots of activities in school
A lways having fun
N ever climb over the gate

Diwan Yogendra (7)
Krishna Avanti Primary School, Evington

All About Jaanav

J aanav is very kind
A dventurous
A ctive
N ever stops eating
A lways has friends
V ery intelligent.

Jaanav Desai (7)
Krishna Avanti Primary School, Evington

History Poem

H istorical people
I ntelligent
S ignificant figures
T udor
O lden days
R eign
Y ears.

Anaiya Mistry (7)
Krishna Avanti Primary School, Evington

Happy Day

H orses are cute
A rt is amazing
P rincesses are beautiful
P olly is a dolly
Y ellow is my favourite colour.

Dhruvi Patel (6)
Krishna Avanti Primary School, Evington

All About Kiana

K ind and caring
I like going to different places
A lways funny
N ice at doing gymnastics
A lways active.

Kiana Mamtora (7)
Krishna Avanti Primary School, Evington

Stars

S tars are beautiful in the sky
T he stars are new stars
A nd stars glow bright
R oyal is gold just like the stars.

Priya Goraniya (7)
Krishna Avanti Primary School, Evington

All About Aron

A ron is my brother
R eading things nicely
O rdering things every day
N ever stop thinking about McDonald's.

Amelia Venugopalan (6)
Krishna Avanti Primary School, Evington

Mavleen's Poem

M arvellous
A lways caring
V ery brave
L oving
E xcellent
E nergetic
N ice.

Mavleen Kaur (7)
Krishna Avanti Primary School, Evington

Kaiyah

K ind
A nice person
I love school
Y ou are my BFF Amelia
A lovely person
H elpful.

Kaiyah Jasmine Patel (6)
Krishna Avanti Primary School, Evington

All About Raina

R aina is brave and strong
A best friend
I am respectful
N ice and kind
A lways working hard.

Raina Bhundia (6)
Krishna Avanti Primary School, Evington

All Describing Me

T ulsi is my name and I'm caring
U nique
L oves everyone
S hy
I have two best friends.

Tulsi Barot (7)
Krishna Avanti Primary School, Evington

Kindness!

K indness is caring
I help people
N ice to people
D o good things.

Mylo Vekaria (7)
Krishna Avanti Primary School, Evington

All About Raj Keshvala

R especting others
A ll about being nice
J ourneys with family.

Raj Keshvala (6)
Krishna Avanti Primary School, Evington

Austin

A Mario Party!
U nhappy when me and Mummy lose
S ometimes I play with toys
T eam game on Mario Party
I imagine a peaceful bath
N ap time at last!

Austin Hughes (10)
Marjorie McClure School, Chislehurst

Cassie

C ats are my favourite
A lways had glasses
S ometimes I am wobbly
S leepy
I am special
E at broccoli and leaves.

Cassandra Weallans (10)
Marjorie McClure School, Chislehurst

Taylor

T aylor likes hamsters
A t breakfast
Y ou like treats
L ay in bed asleep
O pen the cage
R un around the room.

Taylor Blake (8)
Marjorie McClure School, Chislehurst

Saskia

S is for Saskia, that is my name
A is for adventurous, having fun is my aim
S is for smiles, spreading smiles all around
K is for kindness, loving the friends that I've found
I is for inspirational, I'm a brave little girl
A is for artistic, being creative is so much fun.

Saskia Freeman (5)
Montreal CE Primary School, Cleator Moor

Happiness

H appiness is butterflies in the sky
A nd birds singing in the trees
P eople laughing and dancing
P ets running around
I n the park
N o sad faces
E verybody has a big smile
S inging very loudly
S unny days and no rain.

Lucy Gearing (6)
Montreal CE Primary School, Cleator Moor

The Seasons Poem

S pring has blossom trees
E at ice cream in summer
A s the nights get dark winter is here
S un is very hot in summer
O range leaves in autumn
N o leaves in winter
S now falls in winter.

Amelia Nicholson (7)
Montreal CE Primary School, Cleator Moor

Bella

B is for Bella, that is my name
E is for energetic, I love to run around and play
L is for learning, I find this so much fun
L is for my loving family and friends
A is for awesome I do what I enjoy.

Bella Freeman (6)
Montreal CE Primary School, Cleator Moor

Holiday

H ot sunny days
O cean blue
L ilos floating in the water
I ce lollies freeze my brain
D ancing in the sun
A water slide to make you shout, "Wheee!"
Y ippee! Family time.

Keelan Connolly (7)
Montreal CE Primary School, Cleator Moor

Christmas Time

C hilly outside
H ot chocolate
R oast dinner
I n my belly
S now is falling
T insel everywhere
M agic reindeer
A re you asleep yet?
S anta is coming.

Quinn Beeson (6)
Montreal CE Primary School, Cleator Moor

Mopsy

- **M** opsy is my pet rabbit
- **O** utside she hops around
- **P** eacefully she chews on her toys
- **S** ometimes she's naughty and kicks her cage
- **Y** ummy orange carrots are her favourite treat.

Freya Jennings (7)
Montreal CE Primary School, Cleator Moor

Hallie Dog

H airy and soft, the best dog ever
A lways loving and caring
L oyal to us all
L et's remember the good times
I know I will
E ternally loved and missed.

Seth Faragher (6)
Montreal CE Primary School, Cleator Moor

Football

F un sport
O utdoors
O r indoors
T ackling players
B all fumbled
A lways fun
L ots of action
L ots of fun.

Isla Devine (7)
Montreal CE Primary School, Cleator Moor

Harry!

H aving lots of fun
A lways running around with a ball
R unning left
R unning right
Y elling, "Suiiii!" when he scores a goal!

Harry Cope (5)
Montreal CE Primary School, Cleator Moor

Happy Days

H olidays are fun
A t the beach in the sun
P laying in the sand
P eople are having fun in the sea
Y oung kids are playing in the water.

Darcey McCall (6)
Montreal CE Primary School, Cleator Moor

My Favourite Place

E lla loves to play at the play centre
L ots of children laugh and enjoy
L oving the slides and soft play
A super fun day for me and my family!

Ella Gauld (4)
Montreal CE Primary School, Cleator Moor

Brooke Donnell

B rilliant and exciting
R adiant and glowing
O bliging and courteous
O h so good
K ind and caring
E ffervescent.

Brooke Donnell (7)
Montreal CE Primary School, Cleator Moor

Dance

D ancing to get my medals
A lways try my best
N ever give up
C ome on, let's have fun
E veryone loves to dance.

Rosa-Mai Rice (7)
Montreal CE Primary School, Cleator Moor

My Best Friend Rosa

R osa likes to eat grass
O nly in the field she is full of sass
S unshine all around
A nd happiness is of grassy ground.

Esmae-Rose Dawson (5)
Montreal CE Primary School, Cleator Moor

Lambs

L ambs are special
A nd I love them
M y lambs live in a pen
B ottles of milk
S it and feed them.

George Rigg (4)
Montreal CE Primary School, Cleator Moor

I Love Lego

L ego means play
E very day I build
G reen is my favourite colour
O akley loves Lego.

Oakley Pattinson (5)
Montreal CE Primary School, Cleator Moor

Evie

E lephants are big
V ets care for sick pets
I love playing
E veryone is amazing.

Evie Dalton (5)
Montreal CE Primary School, Cleator Moor

Sand

S andy hands
A castle on a hill
N ot enough time
D reaming of a sunny day.

James Finch (7)
Montreal CE Primary School, Cleator Moor

Lola

L aughter and fun
O bliging and helpful
L ittle and precious
A lways kind.

Lola Adams (5)
Montreal CE Primary School, Cleator Moor

Wolf

W olf is big and bad
O range eyes
L ong tail
F rightening everyone.

Reggie Graham (4)
Montreal CE Primary School, Cleator Moor

Emma Nelson

E xcellent Emma
M agnificent convincing skills
M arvellous keyboard player
A bright sister

N o one can replace her
E mma always sticks up for me
L ove all around her
S o much kindness around her
O n bad days she always tries to cheer me up
N o one is like her.

Katie Nelson (7)
St Paul's CE Primary School, Winchmore Hill

Panda Bears

P erfect, pretty pandas
A dorable creatures that
N ever stop eating bamboo
D ark black fur
A mazing climbing animals that

B righten up your day
E xcellent at taking care of each other
A mazing pandas
R olling down the hill and
S mothering themselves in mud.

Sarah Carlotti (7)
St Paul's CE Primary School, Winchmore Hill

My Penguin Posey

P osey is my favourite penguin
E very night I cuddle her in bed
N ever go near a mummy penguin or they'll peck you
G ood job Posey is a baby penguin
U nfortunately, she's not real
I love her, I really do
N ight-time has fallen and Posey is sleeping.

Isabelle Ellis (7)
St Paul's CE Primary School, Winchmore Hill

Vheer

V heer is my name
H onest I am
E xcellent I am
E nthusiastic I am
R ohit is my dad

S uper I am
A rtistic I am
H igh-spirited I am
O is my favourite letter
T reasure is good
A crostic poems are fun.

Vheer Vaswani (6)
St Paul's CE Primary School, Winchmore Hill

An Acrostic Poem About Jacob

J acob is my name
A wesome I am
C ake is the best
O ctopuses are great
B all is my favourite game

K icking balls is fun
A lion is my favourite animal
L icking pancakes is great
U mbrella makes me dry.

Jacob Kalu (6)
St Paul's CE Primary School, Winchmore Hill

Horses Are Wonderful!

H orses are beautiful and friendly.
O n horseback, I feel happy and calm.
R iding is so much fun!
S trong, powerful and elegant creatures.
E ating Polo mints is their favourite treat.
S peedily, horses gallop through the fields.

Phoebe Christofedou (7)
St Paul's CE Primary School, Winchmore Hill

My Family

F reddie is my amazing brother.
A lso, my daddy cooks wonderful meals.
M ummy is helpful, kind and loving.
I sabella is my cousin.
L orraine is Isabella's mummy, my auntie.
Y ou are my family too!

Elizabeth Roberts (7)
St Paul's CE Primary School, Winchmore Hill

Arsenal

A lways scoring goals
R ed is their colour
S mith Rowe is the best
E mirates Stadium is where they play
N oisy crowds singing songs
A ll fans hoping they'll win
L ots of FA Cups.

Joseph Coombes (7)
St Paul's CE Primary School, Winchmore Hill

Spring

S unny spring is here
P retty flowers are standing brightly
R abbits eating carrots
I t's school holidays
N o way I'm doing homework
G reen grass gets cut.

Milo Albery (6)
St Paul's CE Primary School, Winchmore Hill

Easter

E veryone knows it's when Jesus rose
A ll things are bright
S ee lots of family and friends
T ake a nice walk
E at lots of chocolate
R ed flowers so beautiful.

Ezekiel Cawood (7)
St Paul's CE Primary School, Winchmore Hill

Yummy Sweets

S our, sticky, but tasty.
W e all love them so much.
E veryone is tempted.
E ven you!
T wo, three, four, where did they go?
S o yummy, so happy.

Teddy Hale (6)
St Paul's CE Primary School, Winchmore Hill

Summer Fun

S izzling in the sun
U mbrellas up to keep cool
M ake a sandcastle
M ake a picnic lunch
E at up everyone
R un away, it is starting to rain.

Mia Ellis (7)
St Paul's CE Primary School, Winchmore Hill

Beautiful Roses

R uby-red roses
O bviously beautiful roses growing
S cented roses making air smell nice
E legant petals flowing in the wind
S weet-smelling roses.

Emma Nelson (7)
St Paul's CE Primary School, Winchmore Hill

Sonic

S uper Sonic speed
O nly he can run that fast
N ever unkind or bad!
I nfinite is Sonic's ultimate enemy
C an Eggman defeat Sonic?

Austin Reeves (7)
St Paul's CE Primary School, Winchmore Hill

Iris

I 'm a girl's name
R ainbows make me a goddess
I 'm a bright and colourful flower
S ometimes I'm purple, yellow or white.

Iris Lim (7)
St Paul's CE Primary School, Winchmore Hill

Spurs

S on is one of the best
P laying for his team
U nder his feet goes the ball
R unning out of steam
S till trying not to fall.

Josh Jagpal (7)
St Paul's CE Primary School, Winchmore Hill

I Love Dinos

D angerous meat eaters
I guanadons had a spike
N atural history museum
O ceans had dinos too
S pinosaurus had a frill.

Alexander Scott (7)
St Paul's CE Primary School, Winchmore Hill

Tennis

T errific hits
E xciting shots
N early hit the net
N ever easy
I n or out?
S ome friends met.

Finn Davies (7)
St Paul's CE Primary School, Winchmore Hill

Holly

H olly is my name
O pen-minded I am
L icking doughnuts is great
L ovely I am
Y ellow makes me happy.

Holly Bennett (6)
St Paul's CE Primary School, Winchmore Hill

Fifa

F un to play
I support Man City
F un to play with your friends
A mazing game to play, even I play it.

Aston Agyekum (7)
St Paul's CE Primary School, Winchmore Hill

Luke

L uke is my name
U nselfish I am
K ind I am
E nergetic I am.

Luke Mournehis (5)
St Paul's CE Primary School, Winchmore Hill

Fun Stuff

A fun thing
R emarkable picture
T errific paintings.

Nell Taheny (7)
St Paul's CE Primary School, Winchmore Hill

Nervous Noah!

N ervous is not a good feeling
E veryone is nervous at least one time
R arely you don't feel nervous when you start a new school
V ery hard things make me nervous
O vercome your feelings when you're nervous
U sually hard things make me nervous
S ometimes the feelings don't go.

Noah Kessler (7)
The White House Preparatory School, London

Do Not Feel Nervous!

N ervous is a feeling I always feel.
E veryone feels nervous from time to time.
R emember grown-ups get nervous too.
V ery often we feel nervous.
O nce you get nervous, it is hard to go away.
U nderstand yourself.
S how your nerves to other people, don't worry!

Edward Kelsey (7)
The White House Preparatory School, London

Playtime!

P laytime is a good feeling
L aughing with your friends is good
A re you happy or sad... always play!
Y oung and old like to play
F ighting is not playing!
U nited with fabulous friends at playtime
L aughing puts a smile on everybody's face.

Francesca Lombardi-Werner (7)
The White House Preparatory School, London

Playtime!

P lease can it be playtime
L ovely laughs with your friends is better than work
A lways play don't fight
Y oung and old can play together
F abulous friends play in harmony
U se the toys carefully
L aughing is great medicine.

Zixi Jian (7)
The White House Preparatory School, London

Perfect Playtime!

P layful is a good feeling.
L ucky me, it's time to play.
A mazing everyone wants to play with me.
Y oung and old love to play.
F avourite time of the day is playtime!
L oving and playing makes everyone smile!

Nate Sanger (7)
The White House Preparatory School, London

Super Excited!

E xcited is a super feeling
X mas is exciting!
C ome along, be joyful
I n a wonderfully warm place
T oys and gifts, I'm so happy
E veryone needs to be excited at Xmas
D on't stop being excited!

Iris Adeusi (7)
The White House Preparatory School, London

Happy Times!

H appiness is a great feeling
A lways I'm happy when I play football
P eople make me happy when they smile
P lease don't make me blue
Y ay, hooray! It's time to play. Happy times!

Ajit Nair (7)
The White House Preparatory School, London

Happy

H appy is a great feeling
A lways I am happy with my favourite friends
P lease don't make me blue
P ushes or pulls make me sad
Y es I may cry but I'm happy.

Henry Gaunt (7)
The White House Preparatory School, London

Happy Oliver

H appiness is a great feeling
A ll people giggle and laugh when they are happy
P lease don't be sad
P at yourself when you're happy
Y esterday I was happy.

Oliver Xu (7)
The White House Preparatory School, London

Happy Me!

H appiness is great!
A ll day I want to be happy.
P erfect... when I am happy.
P lease don't make me blue.
Y ellow like the sun, it brightens up my day.

Zara Watt (7)
The White House Preparatory School, London

Happy Me!

H appiness is brilliant!
A ll people gloriously giggle!
P lease don't make me so sad
P lease make me ultra happy!
Y esterday I jumped with happiness.

Jai McKenzie (7)
The White House Preparatory School, London

Happy Me!

H appiness is a great feeling
A ll the time you make me happy
P erfect I am horrendously happy
P erfect feelings are great
Y ay, I love being happy.

Mia Aggarwal (7)
The White House Preparatory School, London

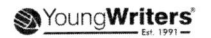

Caring

C aring for people
A pples are my favourite
R eally like writing
I gloos are great
N anny's house is fun
G rowing plants is something I do.

Tia Marley (7)
Wold Newton Foundation School, Wold Newton

Millie

M e and my little sister
I am very caring
L ike playing with my cousins
L ove Mummy, Dad and Evie
I like ice cream
E verything is nice.

Millie Worrell (7)
Wold Newton Foundation School, Wold Newton

Orange

O ther people eating oranges
R eally sweet
A nd very yummy
N ot always my favourite
G ood for your health
E verything is orange.

Noah Pinder (7)
Wold Newton Foundation School, Wold Newton

Green

G reat old green
R eally dark and dangerous
E verywhere I look there is green
E xtremely edible green apples
N ature is sometimes green.

Barnaby Elston (7)
Wold Newton Foundation School, Wold Newton

Beach

B eautiful butterflies
E veryone is playing with me
L ove my lollipops
L ike to lick my chocolate
E veryone likes me.

Isabelle Hunter (7)
Wold Newton Foundation School, Wold Newton

Chloe

C areful Chloe
H appy, smiley Chloe
L ovely, amazing Chloe
O range is my favourite fruit
E xtremely good at maths.

Chloe Warters (6)
Wold Newton Foundation School, Wold Newton

Mummy

M y mummy wears pretty clothes
U n-sad
M y mummy likes eating
M y mummy likes caring
Y ou have yellow hair.

Alban Joyce (7)
Wold Newton Foundation School, Wold Newton

Halo

H i, I am Master Chief
A lso he is dangerous
L ollies are his favourite food
O ranges are his favourite fruit.

Harvey Hart (7)
Wold Newton Foundation School, Wold Newton

Pink

P ink is my favourite colour
I nky is in my reading book
N ice light pink
K ind and caring.

Florence Scott (7)
Wold Newton Foundation School, Wold Newton

Gymnastics

G o on Thursdays
Y ummy drinks
M um watches me
N o shoes or socks
A red mat
S ide splits
T wo trainers
I enjoy it
C artwheels
S plits.

Sophie Hender (6)
Ysgol Ffordd Dyffryn, Llandudno

Swimming

S eahorse costume
W ater
I had fun
M y dad watches me
M y towel
I like to swim
N ew in the class
G etting wet.

Elodie Evans (6)
Ysgol Ffordd Dyffryn, Llandudno

School

S ee my friends at school
C olouring is fun
H ome time
O utside is the best
O n school days I have brechdanau
L ouis is my friend.

Azra Gayrak (6)
Ysgol Ffordd Dyffryn, Llandudno

Fortnite

F ortnite is amazing
O pen doors
R umbling controller
T eams
N ew skins
I can roll
T eammates
E nemies.

Louie Thomas (6)
Ysgol Ffordd Dyffryn, Llandudno

Ballet

B est friend is Darcie
A brother called Leo
L eotard for gymnastics
L ove swimming
E veryone joins in
T utu on my leotard.

Niamh Foster (6)
Ysgol Ffordd Dyffryn, Llandudno

School

S chool is cool
C olouring hurts my hand
H arlem is the best
O f is a red word
O utside has a play road
L ove my friends.

Christopher Jones-Gallagher (6)
Ysgol Ffordd Dyffryn, Llandudno

Kittens

K ittens are cute
I stroke them
T hey scratch
T iny
E liza loves kittens
N ice and soft
S cratch post.

Eliza Trow (5)
Ysgol Ffordd Dyffryn, Llandudno

Alanur

A lanur is my name
L ovely hair
A zra is my friend
N ice hair bobbles
U nder the sea
R ed flowers in my hand.

Alanur Gurel (5)
Ysgol Ffordd Dyffryn, Llandudno

Alice

A lice is my name
L ove Monty and Shan
I like the toy shop
C ruse is my surname
E lodie is my cousin.

Alice Cruse (6)
Ysgol Ffordd Dyffryn, Llandudno

Demi

D ancing is fun
E ating doughnuts is the best
M usic makes me happy
I love my dogs.

Demi Shingler (6)
Ysgol Ffordd Dyffryn, Llandudno

Family

F un
A mazing
M ummy
I love them
L aughing
Y es, I am happy.

Mya Griffiths (6)
Ysgol Ffordd Dyffryn, Llandudno

Billy

B illy is a friend
I like him
L ovely boy
L ots of play
Y ou are kind.

Harlem Williams (6)
Ysgol Ffordd Dyffryn, Llandudno

Young Writers Information

We hope you have enjoyed reading this book – and that you will continue to in the coming years.

If you're the parent or family member of an enthusiastic poet or story writer, do visit **www.youngwriters.co.uk/subscribe** and sign up to receive news, competitions, writing challenges and tips, activities and much, much more! There's lots to keep budding writers motivated!

If you would like to order further copies of this book, or any of our other titles, then please give us a call or order via your online account.

Young Writers
Remus House
Coltsfoot Drive
Peterborough
PE2 9BF
(01733) 890066
info@youngwriters.co.uk

Join in the conversation!
Tips, news, giveaways and much more!

YoungWritersUK   YoungWritersCW   youngwriterscw